This Walker book belongs to:

Amede

Mery Christmas 2017

Love

Aunty Clare 3
                Natty xx

For Kerris and Kitty

First published 1998 by
Walker Books Ltd
87 Vauxhall Walk,
London SE11 5HJ

This edition published 2009

10 9

Illustrations © 1998 Daniel Postgate

The right of Daniel Postgate to be identified as illustrator of this work
has been asserted by him in accordance with the Copyright,
Designs and Patents Act 1988

This book has been typeset in Joe Regular

Printed in China

British Library Cataloguing in Publication Data:

a catalogue record for this book is available from the British Library

ISBN 978-1-4063-2252-1

www.walker.co.uk

The Hairy Toe

Illustrated by

Daniel Postgate

WALKER BOOKS
AND SUBSIDIARIES

LONDON • BOSTON • SYDNEY • AUCKLAND

Once there was a woman went out to pick beans,

and she found ...   a Hairy Toe.

She took the Hairy Toe
home with her,

and that night,
when she went to bed,

the wind began to moan and groan.

Away off in the distance
she seemed to hear
a voice crying,

"Where's my Hair-r-ry To-o-o-oe?
Who's got my Hair-r-ry To-o-o-oe?"

The woman scrooched down,

'way down ...

nder the covers,

and about that time ...

the wind appeared to hit the house, **Sw**

osh, and the old house creaked and cracked like something was trying to get in.

The voice had come
nearer,

almost at the door now,
and it said,

"Where's my
Hair-r-ry To-o-oe?

Who's got my
Hair-r-ry To-o-oe?"

The woman scrooched further down

under the covers

and pulled them tight around her head.

The wind growled around the house
like some big animal and

-r-um-mbled over the chimbley.

All at once she heard the door **cr-r-a-ack**

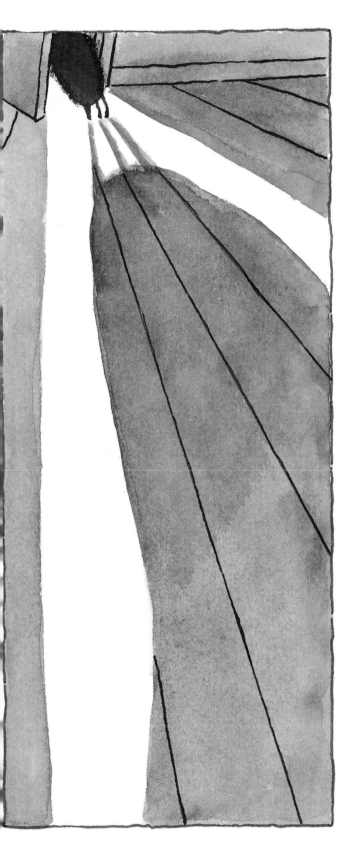

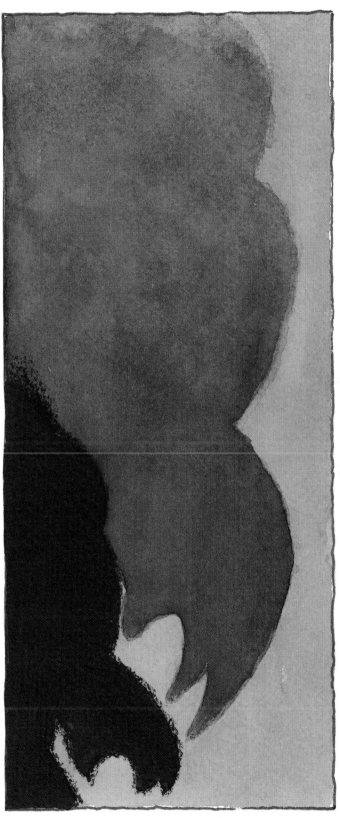

and Something
slipped in

and began to creep
over the floor.

The floor went **cre-e-eak** **cre-e-eak**

at every step that thing took

towards her bed.

The woman could almost feel it bending over her bed.

Then in an awful voice it said:

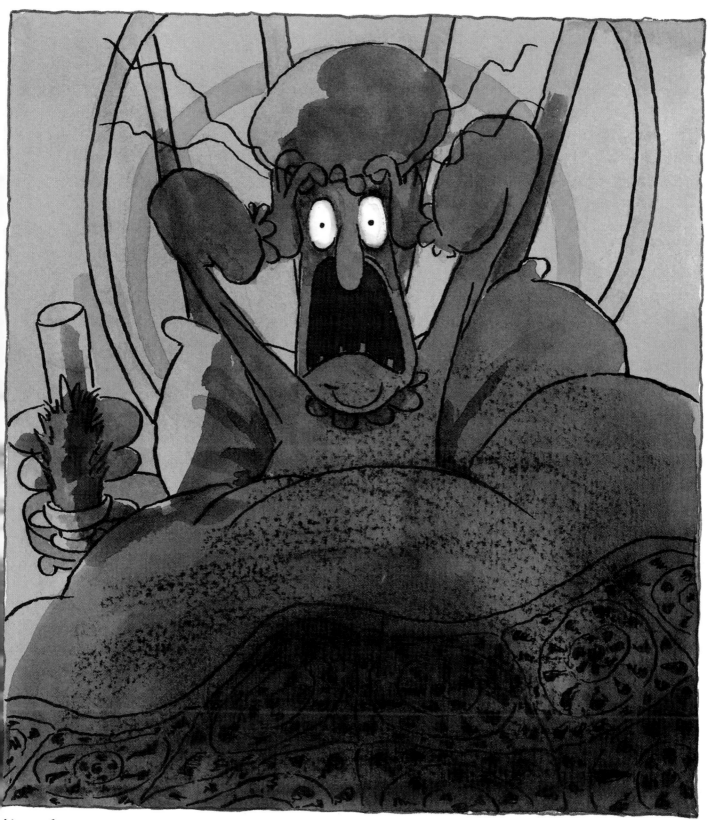

"Where's my Hair-r-ry To-o-oe?
Who's got my Hair-r-ry To-o-oe?"

"You've go

t!"